RAINBOW magic™

Belle the Birthday Fairy was originally published as a Rainbow Magic special. This version has been specially adapted for beginner readers.

Special thanks to
Rachel Elliot and
Fiona Munro

Reading Consultant: Prue Goodwin, lecturer in literacy and children's books.

ORCHARD BOOKS

This story first published in Great Britain in 2013 by Orchard Books
This edition published in 2016 by The Watts Publishing Group

12

HiT entertainment

A CIP catalogue record for this book is available from the British Library.

ISBN 978 1 40832 743 2

Printed in China

The paper and board used in this book are made from wood from responsible sources

Orchard Books
An imprint of Hachette Children's Group
Part of The Watts Publishing Group Limited
Carmelite House, 50 Victoria Embankment, London EC4Y 0DZ

An Hachette UK Company
www.hachette.co.uk
www.hachettechildrens.co.uk

Belle
the Birthday Fairy

by Daisy Meadows

ORCHARD

www.rainbowmagic.co.uk

The Fairyland Palace

Fairy Houses

Fields

Bakery

Tippington Town

BAKERY

Jack Frost's
Ice Castle

Road to Ice
Castle

Village
Hall

Rachel's
House

Skate Park

Story One

The Birthday Book

The Birthday Book

"I can't wait to see Mum's face when she arrives at her surprise party!" Rachel Walker said as she and her best friend, Kirsty Tate, happily swung their roller skates on their way to the park.

"She'll be amazed when she realises that you and your dad have arranged it all!" Kirsty grinned. She was staying at Rachel's house in Tippington for half-term, and for the party.

"Everything's ready," Rachel went on, "the food, the music,

the decorations for the village hall. And Dad's ordered a cake from the baker's."

As they passed the village hall, where the party was to be held, Rachel squeezed Kirsty's hand. "Let's quickly look inside," she said.

"Ooh, yes!" replied Kirsty eagerly, and they put their heads around the door.

A group of party guests were there, but no one was having much fun. The parents were clearing up squashed cakes and spilled drinks, and instead of playing music, the CD player was making strange whining sounds. Rachel and Kirsty looked around, and saw a little girl in a pink dress looking sad.

"Is this your party?" Rachel asked her.

"Yes." She nodded sadly. "But everything's gone wrong. We can't even dance!"

The two older girls tried their best to comfort her.

When they got to the park, the girls put on their skates. But they both still felt upset about the little girl's party being ruined.

"If only one of the Party Fairies had been here, they could have helped." Kirsty sighed. The girls were good friends with the fairies, often helping them outwit bad-tempered Jack Frost and his naughty goblin servants.

"You're right!" said a musical voice close by. Peering into a hedge, the girls saw a tiny fairy sitting cross-legged. She had long brown hair and was wearing a pretty purple dress, with sparkly gold ballet pumps.

"Hi, girls!" She smiled. "I'm Belle the Birthday Fairy, and I need your help!"

"Hi, Belle!" said Rachel and Kirsty together. "What's wrong?"

"Jack Frost has stolen my birthday charms, and we must get them back!"

Belle explained that the birthday charms make sure birthdays go smoothly in

Fairyland and the human world. With the charms in Jack Frost's hands, birthdays everywhere were going wrong.

"Will you come to Fairyland and help me search for clues?" asked Belle.

"Of course!" the girls cried together.

Belle waved her wand and multicoloured sparkles spun all around them. A few moments later, they were floating over Fairyland.

As they fluttered above

emerald-green hills, Kirsty
became curious about

the birthday charms they
were looking for and Belle
explained. "The birthday book
contains everyone's birthday.
Without it nobody knows

when birthdays are!" The girls nodded as Belle went on. "The birthday candle makes all birthday cakes delicious and grants wishes. The birthday present makes sure everyone receives the perfect gift."

"Without those charms, nobody will ever have a happy birthday again!" said Rachel.

She looked very glum.

"That's why Jack Frost stole them!" cried Belle. "It's his birthday soon, and he's feeling really miserable about his age and wants everyone else to be miserable too!"

"How mean!" said Kirsty.

As they flew over the glittering Fairyland Palace, Kirsty saw something. "Look!" she exclaimed.

Far below they could see three goblins scrambling up a ladder and into the palace!

"They're up to mischief!" said Belle. "Let's see if we can find out what's going on!"

Belle and the girls zoomed through the back door of the palace. Turning a corner, they watched as the pesky goblins tiptoed into the palace library.

"What if this has something to do with the birthday charms?" whispered Rachel. "Let's creep in and listen to what they're saying."

The fairies fluttered silently into the cosy library.

"Look!" whispered Rachel as they ducked behind an armchair. The goblins were pulling books from shelves and throwing them on the floor.

"Hurry up!" a tall goblin

hissed. "We need to know when Jack Frost's birthday is so we can plan his surprise party!"

The girls stared at each other. The birthday book was hidden here in the Palace Library!

"The goblins want the book

as much as we do," Kirsty realised. "Let's try and persuade them to help us!" She got up.

"We overheard what you said about the party," Kirsty began bravely. "You need that book as much as we do." The goblins whirled around in surprise.

"We'll let you stay and look up Jack Frost's birthday, if you promise to return the book to Belle," added Rachel.

The frowning goblins huddled together and, after lots

of muffled arguing, they agreed. The search went on and on, while outside the library the sun began to set.

At last, when every shelf had been searched, they pulled the cushions off the chairs. And there it was!

"I've got it!" yelled the smallest goblin.

The little goblin waved the shining book above his head, but it flew out of his hands and landed safely in Belle's arms.

As Belle turned the

shimmering pages of the
birthday book, the goblins
spotted Jack Frost's name. They
found his birthday on the list
and scurried off.

"Thanks for helping me find this!" said Belle to the girls. "But it's time you two returned to the human world."

Belle smiled as she flicked her wand. There was a whoosh of rainbow-coloured sparkles.

When Kirsty and Rachel opened their eyes again they were back in the human world.

"I can't wait for our next fairy adventure!" smiled Kirsty.

Story Two

The Birthday Candle

The Birthday Candle

"I hope it stops raining before Mum's surprise party on Saturday," said Rachel. She and Kirsty were at the bakery to collect Mrs Walker's birthday cake. They were looking at the yummy treats in the window.

Inside the bakery, delicious smells filled the air.

"We've come to collect the birthday cake for Mrs Walker," Rachel said to the baker behind the counter.

"Oh dear," he replied sadly. "I'm having terrible trouble with that cake." Behind him, the girls could see what he meant.

There sat a wonky cake with icing sliding off and sticky decorations lying beside it.

Suddenly, Kirsty tugged on Rachel's arm. "We'll come back tomorrow," she said, walking out of the shop.

"Why are we leaving so quickly?" asked Rachel, surprised.

"Because of what I've just seen at the window!" Kirsty whispered urgently.

Back outside, Kirsty pointed at three people who were crowding under one small umbrella. All three of them were wearing wellies. But Rachel looked again when she realised that above the wellies, she could see green legs!

"They're goblins!" she gasped. The girls stared in amazement at the silly green creatures. The goblins scurried into the

bakery, splashing rainwater
everywhere.

"I don't know what they're
doing here," said Kirsty, "but
we're getting soaked!"

And as Kirsty raised her
umbrella above their heads,
it began to glow inside like a
glitter ball!

"Belle!" smiled Kirsty as
the tiny fairy spiralled down
the handle. "Thank goodness
you're here! Three goblins have
just gone into the bakery."

"I know," said Belle,
unhappily. "I'm sure they're
planning some mischief."

"We came to collect Mum's cake," said Rachel, "but it's all wonky."

Belle sighed. "No birthday cakes will bake properly until we find the missing birthday candle charm."

"Belle, could you turn us into fairies?" asked Kirsty. "We must find out what those goblins are up to."

With a wave of Belle's wand and a flurry of sparkles, the girls shrank to fairy-size.

The bakery door was ajar, so

the three fairies slipped inside and watched as the baker brought out cake after cake to show the goblins.

"These just aren't good enough!" said the tallest one.

"Boring!" shouted the middle goblin, poking a bony finger into a cake.

"But this is my best selection!" cried the baker.

"Ha!" snorted the tallest goblin. "We're from the Cake Standards Board, and we'll shut this bakery down unless you start making better ones!"

"We could make better cakes than this standing on our heads!" yelled the middle goblin.

"Get out!" screeched the smallest goblin to the confused baker.

"Go! Go! GO!" added the

middle goblin. He gave the
baker an umbrella and pushed
him towards the door.

"I suppose I could take my
lunch break now." The poor
baker watched as the goblins
locked the door behind him.

"Why are they being so horrible?" asked Rachel.

"Let's find out!" said Belle. She fluttered after the goblins as they disappeared into the kitchen at the back of the shop.

The goblins were running around the kitchen spilling flour and breaking eggs.

"Oh, no!" Kirsty exclaimed. "They're wrecking the place!"

"I think they're trying to make a cake!" said Belle as they watched the goblins stir ingredients in a mixing bowl.

"Stop shoving me!" squawked one of the goblins, as he broke an egg over another's head.

"Shut up and fetch the candle!" the tallest goblin

snapped. The middle one stomped over to the pile of coats and pulled a beautiful shimmering cake candle out of one of the pockets.

"That's it!" said Belle. "That's my birthday candle charm!"

The goblins were still arguing and crashing around the kitchen. Just then, Rachel saw the one holding the candle add a large spoonful of chilli powder to the bowl.

"That's going to taste horrible!" she whispered.

At last, the goblin put the candle down on the worktop. He turned to put his cake into the oven. Rachel gulped, then flew down and grabbed the candle, just as the goblin turned back again!

"It's one of those pesky fairies!" he cried, grabbing a sieve and bringing it crashing down on top of Rachel. She was trapped!

"Goblins, give me the candle and let Rachel go!" insisted Belle, swooping down.

"Shan't!" snapped the tallest goblin.

"Does Jack Frost know you're here?" asked Kirsty.

The goblins went pale green. "No, we want his birthday cake to be a surprise!" said the smallest goblin in a trembling voice.

So that's what they were doing! thought Kirsty. "Without magic," she explained, "your cake will take hours to cook. And the baker will be back soon. If you help US, Belle can speed everything up a bit to help YOU!"

The goblins pulled faces at each other before nodding in agreement.

Belle waved her wand and the finished cake floated out of the oven. It landed safely on the table.

"It's horrible!" gasped Kirsty.

"It's spectacular!" grinned the goblins.

The cake was grey, ugly and misshapen. Perfect for Jack Frost.

The middle goblin lifted the sieve and Rachel made her escape. Belle flew down and picked up the birthday candle. She waved her wand over the cake. In a sparkle of magic it was transformed into Jack Frost's face, and topped with large candles. The goblins grabbed it, without bothering to say thank

you, and rushed out of the
door.

Belle flicked her wand, and
the whole room shimmered.
When the sparkles faded,

the kitchen gleamed. A cake decorated with pink icing and pink hearts was sitting on the worktop.

"Perfect!" Rachel cried.

Outside, Belle returned Rachel and Kirsty to their human size. "Thanks to you two, birthday cakes and wishes are safe!" she said.

Belle disappeared in a flurry of fairy dust, clutching the precious birthday candle.

"I hope we can find the last missing birthday charm before

Mum's party!" said Rachel.

"I just know we can!" Kirsty grinned.

Story Three

The Birthday
Present

The Birthday Present

"Surprise!" everyone shouted.

Balloons flew into the air and party poppers rained colourful streamers over the astonished Mrs Walker.

"What a wonderful surprise!"

She smiled as guests wished her a happy birthday.

"Everything's going really well," Kirsty said in a low voice. "I was afraid that Jack Frost would spoil it because he's still got Belle's birthday present charm."

"That reminds me – it's time to give Mum her special gift!" said Rachel in excitement. "It's a jewellery box. I can't wait to see her face when she opens it!"

The two girls and Mr Walker handed the gift to Mrs Walker,

who carefully undid the wrapping paper.

"Oh," she exclaimed, her face falling, as instead of a beautiful jewellery box, she found a pair of muddy old boots inside.

"It's not fair!" Rachel whispered to Kirsty. "Mum would have loved that jewellery box!" Beckoning Kirsty to follow her, she hurried outside and put her hand on the magical locket around her neck. The king and queen of Fairyland had given a locket full of fairy dust to each of the girls. They could use them to go to Fairyland in an emergency.

"We must help Belle find her birthday present charm!" Rachel said.

They sprinkled sparkling
dust from their lockets over
their heads. A glittering whirl
tumbled them through the air
towards Fairyland.

The fairy-sized girls found themselves inside the Fairyland Palace. It didn't take long to find Belle and describe what had happened at the party. Belle sighed and led them to the king and queen. They explained that all the preparations for Jack Frost's own surprise party were going wrong. All because he had hidden the birthday present somewhere in his Ice Castle!

"We could go to the Ice Castle and hunt for it!" Rachel

offered at once.

"We want to help!" Kirsty
agreed.

"Belle can go with you,
but watch out," warned King
Oberon. "It could be very
dangerous."

The three fairies gazed up at Jack Frost's gleaming, icy home, wondering how they were ever going to get inside. Goblin guards were everywhere.

"Look!" cried Kirsty as she spied a goblin zooming towards

the castle on a motorbike pulling a trailer. Quick as a flash, Belle, Rachel and Kirsty hid themselves in the trailer. They rumbled along the icy road until the engine was turned off. Then they heard the goblin walking away. They had made it!

The three brave fairies fluttered out and along a cold, gloomy corridor until they reached a door with "Great Hall" carved above it.

The girls darted into the hall

and began their frantic search under tablecloths and behind curtains. But there were no presents, only cobwebs and woodlice!

Jack Frost's magnificent ice throne stood on a platform in the centre of the room. Eventually, Rachel crouched down behind it and discovered a space underneath. It was full of beautifully wrapped gifts! They pulled them out one by one until Rachel found a tiny box, wrapped in pink paper.

"It's much sparklier than the others," she said.

"That's because it's my birthday present charm!" whispered Belle, her eyes shining with excitement.

Suddenly, the girls heard babbling goblin voices.

"Quick!" cried Kirsty. "Let's get back to the palace!"

Belle waved her wand, but nothing happened.

"Jack Frost must have put a spell on the room," she

explained. "My magic doesn't work. And if we can't return the birthday present to the Fairyland Palace, the goblins' party preparations won't work either!"

Rachel gazed up at the windows. One of them was open.

Belle saw what Rachel was thinking. "We can't fly out of

there," she whispered. "The goblins would grab us."

"Not if they're distracted," replied Rachel with a smile.

Belle looked worried but there was no other way to return the birthday present.

"Hey, goblins! Over here!" shouted a brave Kirsty. The silly green creatures howled with anger and chased the fairies. None of them saw Belle slip out of the window.

Rachel and Kirsty flitted around the hall, dodging

the goblins' grabbing hands.
One jumped onto another's
shoulders and tried to
grab Rachel. But she did a
somersault in mid-air. The
goblin lost his balance and
crashed to the floor with a yell.

"Fairies! WHAT IS GOING ON?" roared Jack Frost from the doorway of the Great Hall. He looked at the chaos all around.

"The goblins are trying to throw you a birthday party," said the gentle voice of Queen Titania. She had arrived just in time.

With a wave of the queen's wand, the Great Hall was transformed into a sparkling party scene. The surprised Jack Frost was even more shocked when three goblins singing "Happy Birthday" carried in the cake with a picture of his face on!

It was the best party ever held at the Ice Castle. As night fell, Queen Titania beckoned to Rachel and Kirsty.

"Thanks to you, we were able to show Jack Frost that birthdays can be fun," said the queen. "Now, I believe you have another party to attend!"

Belle hugged Rachel and Kirsty goodbye as a whirl of glittering fairy dust surrounded them. When the sparkles faded, they were back at Tippington Village Hall. They were just in time to see Mrs Walker opening her beautiful jewellery box.

"It's the perfect present!" said Kirsty.

"But no gift could be better than the adventure we've just had!" Rachel smiled.

**If you enjoyed this story,
you may want to read**

Summer the Holiday Fairy
Early Reader

Here's how the story begins...

It was the start of the summer
holidays. Rachel, her best
friend Kirsty and their parents
were all heading off to
Rainspell Island.

"Have you finished packing
yet?" Mrs Walker called.

"Almost!" Rachel replied.

Rachel and Kirsty had met

on Rainspell Island two years before and had an amazing secret. They were friends with the fairies and had shared so many adventures. Maybe they would have one on this holiday?

"Oh no!" Rachel groaned, pulling her favourite T-shirt from under her bed. It was dirty! Sighing, she went to get her washbag. When she came back she gasped. The T-shirt was sparkly clean! Bending closer, she saw a tiny, glowing footprint on the sleeve. "Fairy dust!" she breathed.

A car beeped outside. Kirsty and her parents had arrived! Rachel rushed downstairs.

"Sorry we're late!" Kirsty's mum said. "The car had a flat tyre when we got up this morning."

"But by the time I'd fetched my tools, it wasn't flat any more." Mr Tate laughed. "Almost like magic!"

Rachel and Kirsty looked at each other. "Kirsty, come and see my new duvet cover before we go," Rachel suggested. She was bursting to tell Kirsty what had happened.

The girls raced upstairs as Rachel's words tumbled out. "I bet your car tyre was fixed by magic," she whispered. "A fairy's been here too!"

Read
Summer the Holiday Fairy
Early Reader
to find out
what happens next!

Learn to read with

RAINBOW magic™

- ♥ Rainbow Magic Early Readers are easy-to-read versions of the original books

- ♥ Perfect for parents to read aloud and for newly confident readers to read along

- ♥ Remember to enjoy reading together. It's never too early to share a story!

Everybody loves Daisy Meadows!

'I love your books' – Jasmine, Essex

'You are my favourite author' – Aimee, Surrey

'I am a big fan of Rainbow Magic!' – Emma, Hertfordshire

Meet the first
Rainbow Magic fairies

Let the magic begin!

RAINBOW magic™

Become a

Rainbow Magic

fairy friend and be the first to
see sneak peeks of new books.

There are lots of special offers and exclusive
competitions to win sparkly
Rainbow Magic prizes.

Sign up today at
www.rainbowmagicbooks.co.uk